Robert Louis Stevenson wrote Treasure Island *in 1881, when he was 31 years old. The story started out as a game of pirates with his young stepson Lloyd during a summer in Scotland's Grampian Mountains and was originally published as a multi-part serial in a children's magazine. It went on to become one of the world's most beloved adventure books.*

Treasure Island *was one of our favorite books when we were kids, and we hope that this dog-eared condensation will entertain our young readers and inspire them to read the original text when they are older.*

John Bianchi
Frank B. Edwards

Dedicated to Buffy (1976-89)
and Molly (1984-98)

Written by Frank B. Edwards
Illustrated by John Bianchi
Copyright 1999 by Pokeweed Press

Cataloguing in Publication Data

Edwards, Frank B., 1952-
    Treasure Island with lots of dogs

(Dog-eared classics series)
Illustrated condensation of Treasure Island, by Robert Louis Stevenson

ISBN 0-894323-11-4 (bound)   ISBN 0-921285-10-6 (pbk.)

    I. Bianchi, John   II. Stevenson, Robert Louis, 1850-1894
III. Title.   IV. Series.

PS8559.D84T74 1999   jC813'.54   C99-900264-3
PZ7.E2535Tr 1999

Published in North America by:
Pokeweed Press
17 Elk Court, Suite 200
Kingston, Ontario
K7M 7A4

Visit Pokeweed Press on the Net at:
www.Pokeweed.com

Send E-mail to Pokeweed Press at:
mail@pokeweed.com

Printed in Canada by:
Friesens Corporation

American sales and marketing by:
Stoddart Kids
a division of Stoddart Publishing Co. Ltd.
180 Varick Street, 9th Floor
New York, New York 10014

Canadian sales and marketing by:
General Publishing
34 Lesmill Road
Toronto, ON
M3B 2T6

Visit General Publishing on the Net at:
www.genpub.com

Distributed in the U.S.A. by:
General Distribution Services
Suite 202
85 River Rock Drive
Buffalo, NY   14207

Distributed in Canada by:
General Distribution Services
325 Humber College Blvd.
Toronto, ON
M9W 7C3

Treasure Island

WITH LOTS OF DOGS

*Based on the classic tale by
Robert Louis Stevenson*

Written by
F r a n k   B .   E d w a r d s

Illustrated by
J o h n   B i a n c h i

My name is Jim Hawkins, and the story I am about to tell you took place when I was just a pup. While I promised my shipmates that I would record the full details of our dangerous voyage, I cannot reveal the exact location of Treasure Island, for there is still booty awaiting our return.

My adventure began the day the mysterious Captain Billy Bones slunk through our door at the Admiral Bed & Bone Inn, looking for a glass of rum and a warm bed. With four small pieces of gold, he paid for a month's lodging — and changed our lives forever.

Every day, he paced the cliffs of our rocky cove with his brass spyglass, and every night, he sat by a window lapping rum and staring out at the road as if waiting for someone. At the start of each month, he gave me a silver coin if I promised to watch for "a seafaring swab missing one leg."

Some nights, after too much rum, he would loudly tell stories of his life at sea and would force the other lodgers to join him in a tuneless verse of a wretched old sea shanty:

Fifteen bones on a dead dog's chest
Arf-arf-arf and a bottle of rum!

Everyone at the inn was frightened of Billy Bones, and we prayed for the day when he would leave, for he seldom paid his bills. But it seemed that nothing could encourage him to move on.

I promised to watch for "a seafaring swab missing one leg."

We had nearly given up hope of ever ridding ourselves of our unwelcome guest, when a blind beggar arrived one day with a message for Billy Bones. As the captain looked up from his grog, the dirty dog passed him a small piece of paper that bore a crudely drawn black spot.

His cruel job done, the messenger felt his way out the door and disappeared into the fog, leaving Billy Bones staring at the evil-looking dot.

"It's a death warrant. My time is up," he yelped. "Those sea dogs will be here by midnight to murder us all and steal my map."

Struggling to stand up, the terrified sailor took a short breath, clutched at his heart and fell stone-cold dead — a victim of fear, rum and a life at sea.

Worried for my own safety, I raced to the captain's room and searched his sea chest. I am not a thief, but Billy Bones owed us dearly for his lodging, and I dug until I found some coins and a tattered map. I fetched my mother, and we hurried down the road to the house of Dr. Livesey.

The doctor was eating dinner that night with his wealthy friend Squire Trelawney, but food was soon forgotten as they listened to my story. Unfolding the chart, the two friends declared it to be the treasure map of a famous dead pirate named Captain Flint.

"Well, what say we head for Bristol?" spluttered the squire. "In a few days, we shall have a ship and favorable winds blowing us to this island."

"Aye," said I, looking imploringly toward my mother. "I'm with you."

"As am I," agreed the doctor, "but we must all be as silent as the grave."

Food was soon forgotten when I showed them the map.

Several weeks later, I took leave of my tearful mother and set off with Dr. Livesey for the port of Bristol. Squire Trelawney had gone ahead to secure a seaworthy ship and a trusty crew, and by the time we arrived at the docks, he had purchased a sturdy schooner called the *Hispaniola* and had begun gathering our provisions.

He was delighted to see us and told us excitedly about his luck in finding an experienced crew. As we boarded a skiff and rowed out to inspect the *Hispaniola*, he described an unexpected stroke of good fortune.

"I was standing at dockside last week," he said, "when I was approached by an old sailor who had hobbled down for a whiff of the fresh salt air. Long John Silver was his name. He walked with a crutch — for he had lost a leg in service to the Queen — and he carried a green parrot on his shoulder.

"As we stood admiring the ship, Silver told me that life on shore was bad for his health and that he wanted to head back to sea as a cook. Out of pure pity, I hired him on the spot."

The squire's generosity was instantly rewarded, for Long John seemed to know all the sailors in Bristol, and in no time, he had helped assemble a rough-and-tough pack of old sea dogs. To be sure, they were a mangy-looking crew, with more fleas than manners, but Long John assured the squire that they were ready for adventure.

Long John Silver seemed to know all the sailors in Bristol.

We spent the rest of the day and night laying in supplies, and at dawn's first light, we weighed anchor, caught the wind in our sails and slipped gently out to sea. Our voyage to Treasure Island was finally under way!

Alas, though, there was a sour note sounded that first day by Dr. Livesey. He was not impressed by the crew and was angry that the sailors seemed to know of our quest for buried treasure.

"There has been too much yapping," the doctor growled to Squire Trelawney. "Even Silver's parrot knows about our map by now."

The squire meekly handed the precious map over to Dr. Livesey, and we all agreed to guard our secret more carefully. With that unpleasantness behind us, we set about our tasks.

My job was in the galley with Long John, preparing food and serving the crew. It was hard work, but Long John made the days pass quickly with his tales of life at sea. Everyone aboard had a deep respect for him, and I was sure he could have been a captain instead of a cook. He was kind to everyone and was easily the most popular dog aboard.

"Come and have a yarn with old John," he would say, feeding the parrot and stoking his pipe. "Nobody is more welcome than you, my pup."

He claimed that the parrot was 200 years old and that he had named it Captain Flint after the famous pirate. Remembering the doctor's concern, I knew it was best not to tell Long John that we were actually sailing in search of Captain Flint's gold.

"Come and have a yarn with old John," he would say.

The *Hispaniola* proved to be a good ship, and our outward voyage to Treasure Island went quickly. The winds were fair, and the crew seemed both competent and eager to fulfill its duties. But as we drew close to our destination, I stumbled upon a plot that proved we had unknowingly placed ourselves in great danger.

It was a quiet evening with a steady wind, and I had gone on deck to grab a snack from the biscuit barrel. But the barrel was almost empty, and I had to climb right inside to secure my treat. Tired after a long day in the galley, I curled up in the bottom of the barrel with a couple of biscuits and let the rhythm of the ship lull me to sleep.

I was abruptly awakened by a pair of angry and greedy voices. As I heard the word "treasure," I peered through a bunghole in the huge barrel.

"I'll say when we strike," bristled Long John to his companion. "They have the map, and that means they can keep their tails — at least until they have stowed *our* treasure safely below these decks."

"But then the lads and I will have our fun," snarled Israel Paws, the coxswain. My pounding heart skipped a beat as I realized that the squire had hired a crew of murderous brutes who planned to rob and kill us.

But before Israel Paws could finish his sentence, the lookout barked, "Land ho!"

As the two mutineers howled in delight, I slipped quietly away.

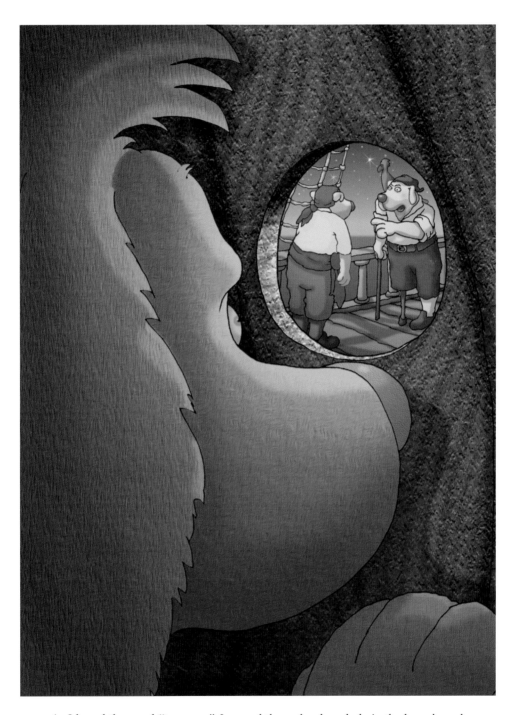

As I heard the word "treasure," I peered through a bunghole in the huge barrel.

While the crew celebrated our first view of Treasure Island, I raced to Dr. Livesey's cabin to give the doctor and the squire my dreadful news. As we spoke, I could hear the sounds of the crew's boisterous songs echoing above our heads:

Fifteen bones on a dead dog's chest
Arf-arf-arf and a bottle of rum!

"I've made a fine mess of things," whimpered the squire. "My first-class crew turned out to be a pack of unruly mongrels."

"This is no time for mournful words," growled the doctor. "We must have a plan. Even with our loyal servants, we are far outnumbered by those grog-fogged sea dogs, but by how much, we do not know."

He then encouraged us to go about our duties as if we were unaware of the mutiny. Once we had determined who was true to our side, we would surprise the pirates when an opportunity presented itself. Until then, we would quietly lock away all the weapons and keep a careful watch.

The next morning, there was no wind and the *Hispaniola* lay becalmed near the mouth of a small bay. The crew seemed to have turned surly overnight and grumbled through the morning chores until Dr. Livesey finally ordered Long John to take two of the longboats ashore for an afternoon's relaxation.

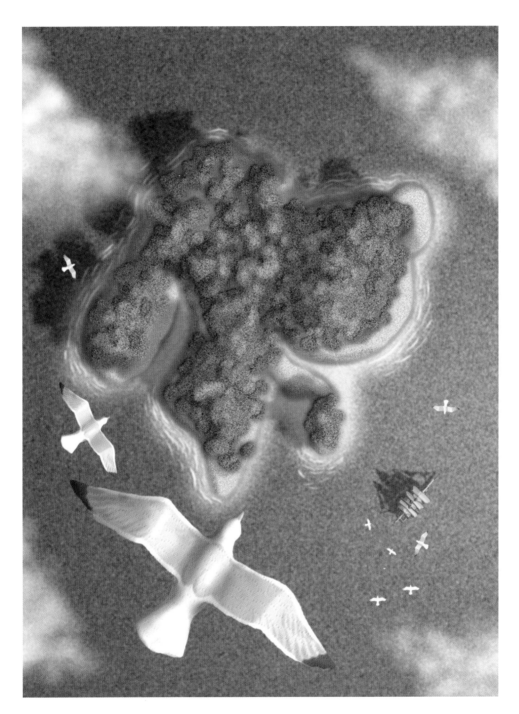

The Hispaniola *lay becalmed near the mouth of a small bay.*

The mood of the crew improved immediately as the sailors prepared to go ashore. As Dr. Livesey had hoped, Long John selected only his mutinous companions for the trip. Of the 10 crew members he left aboard the *Hispaniola*, four seemed loyal to our cause, but the other six were members of his dastardly pack — secretly assigned to keep watch on Squire Trelawney and Dr. Livesey.

Alas, the idea of getting off the ship for a few hours that day inspired me to do something I quickly came to regret.

As the two small boats moved away from the ship, I bounded into one without permission, thinking that I would be a useful spy amongst the pirates. But when I glanced back at the ship and saw a look of despair darken Dr. Livesey's face, I realized that my rash act had been a mistake. Even if my friends could overpower the pirates left aboard the ship, Long John would simply take me hostage. Looking about at the evil curs around me, I knew that I had better try to escape at the first opportunity.

And so it was that the moment the longboat struck the beach, I jumped from the bow and darted into the dense undergrowth near the water's edge. Long John snarled orders to his crew, but I was lost to his eyes before the first pirates had gotten clear of the boats. Not knowing which way I had gone, they stumbled about for some time, barking up the wrong trees while I made my way deeper into the jungle.

The moment the longboat struck the beach, I jumped from the bow.

I ran for perhaps a mile, not daring to look back. When I finally stopped to rest, I was startled to discover that I had been followed by a wild-haired stranger with tattered clothes and crazed eyes.

"My name is Ben Gunn," he panted. "And it's been three long years since I last saw another hound. I was left here to die by a pirate named Flint — and, if I'm not mistaken, some of those sea dogs who are chasing you were part of his cutthroat crew."

While he begged for passage back to Bristol, I explained my own precarious situation. Pawing me feverishly, old Ben promised to help defeat the pirates in exchange for his safe return home.

He then led me down a path to a small hidden beach where he kept a primitive canoe. He urged me to bring my friends to him, but before I could respond, he had disappeared into the trees.

Meanwhile, back on the ship, Dr. Livesey had formed a plan.

"Well," he barked, "if there was wind for our sails, we could leave this cursed place right now while Silver is busy ashore. But, instead, we must move to the safety of an old stockade on the island. It will be easier to defend than this schooner, and I mean to find it before those scoundrels do."

And so, while Israel Paws and the other unarmed pirates watched helplessly, the doctor's crew filled the last longboat with food and weapons and rowed swiftly to Treasure Island.

I was startled to discover that I had been followed by a wild-haired stranger.

Dr. Livesey's luck lasted just long enough to get his small band safely inside the walls of the abandoned fort, but within minutes of their arrival, cannonballs began to whistle overhead.

"Thunderation," growled the squire. "We left the cannons behind for them to use against us."

"Yes," chuckled the doctor. "But so long as they have more rum than gunpowder, we should be all right."

Within an hour, the heroic defense preparations at the fort were interrupted by the arrival of Long John Silver — sporting a white flag atop a sword.

The brave Dr. Livesey cautiously stepped forward.

"So you have come to surrender already?" he sneered.

"Nay, I come to offer a trade," grinned Long John. "In exchange for the map and treasure, we will let you keep your lives."

"A trade?" repeated the doctor. "I will trade you all right — a fair trial in Bristol for your surrender today, you scurvy dog."

And with that, he turned his back on the scowling pirate.

Furious, Long John threw down his flag and hopped back into the jungle. He was barely out of range when the pirates launched a furious attack.

Armed with weapons they had hidden aboard the ship, the mutineers clambered over the stockade walls and tried to storm the blockhouse that sheltered my friends, but they were met by heavy musket fire.

The mutineers clambered over the stockade walls.

For my part, I had paced all afternoon, unsure of what to do. The skull and crossbones was flying above our lovely schooner, so I knew that the *Hispaniola* had fallen into enemy hands, but I was unsure whether my friends were still aboard or had escaped to the island.

The first cannon blast gave me my answer and ended my indecision.

As I watched in horror, the guns were fired repeatedly toward the island against my unseen friends. With no clear plan in mind, I launched Ben Gunn's canoe, hoping that I might somehow be able to stop the bombardment.

I carefully circled behind the ship, but long before I had reached its stern, the cannons had stopped firing. As I came alongside, Long John's attack on the fort must have started, for the howls and shots of battle drifted eerily across the water.

The deck seemed empty when I finally crept aboard, so I made my way to the main mast, thinking that a climb to the crow's nest would give me a clear view of the situation on the island. I was almost to the top of the rigging and had just caught sight of the small island stockade when I heard a commotion down below.

"So the little lubber has come back for treats," cackled Israel Paws, scrambling toward me. "Well, I've got a fine bit of cutlery for you."

Fearing for my life, I grabbed the lookout's pistols from the rack in the crow's nest and fired quickly, sending the old salt to a watery grave.

"So the little lubber has come back for treats," cackled Israel Paws.

As I dashed down the mast, the shooting on the island ended and I happily observed that the ship's Union Jack still fluttered over the fort. My friends were safe for now, and I determined to make them safer.

I decided to cut the ship free of its anchors and let it drift around the tip of the island to Gunn's secret beach. With luck, the pirates would not find it there and I could make my way to the stockade to join the doctor and the squire. If the winds were fair the next day, we could leave the cursed island and head for home.

My plan went well, but it was dark by the time I steered the *Hispaniola* onto the sand. A weak moon and the faint scent of Ben's trail guided me toward the fort, but I took each step in fear of being discovered by the pirates.

Much to my surprise, the outer walls of the stockade had been left unguarded, and I could hear the snores of my sleeping shipmates in the unlit blockhouse. Wishing not to disturb them, I crept quietly inside and curled up in a corner. I was asleep within seconds and dreaming of home until a rough paw shook me awake.

"So, young Hawkins, you decided to sign on with us after all," coughed a familiar voice. "Well, I think we can put you to good use."

And, with a deep growl, Long John Silver gave me a hard poke with his crutch while a leash was slipped over my head.

"So, young Hawkins, you decided to rejoin us," coughed a familiar voice.

L ong John was most amused and howled heartily at my predicament. "Oh, yes, your good doctor won the first round yesterday," he roared. "But there were too few hounds to protect such a fine big yard, and the bunch of them slipped into the woods last night, leaving us to enjoy their food, their map . . . and their visitors."

The whole crew was yipping at Long John's joke when I heard the clear voice of Dr. Livesey outside the stockade. The old pirate hauled me to my feet and led me outside to investigate.

The kindly doctor had come to offer first aid to the wounded pirates and to try again to negotiate their surrender, but Long John had other plans.

"As you can see, sir," he snarled, "we now have a hostage and are preparing to take him on a little treasure hunt of our own. I would be obliged if you allowed us safe passage across the island."

"You will be safer than you deserve," the doctor agreed. "But be warned, Long John Silver, that map will only bring you unhappiness today. I also recommend you protect young Jim with your life."

With that curious warning, he was gone, leaving us to start our expedition. The pirates bounded through the jungle like mindless pups until they stumbled upon one of Captain Flint's weather-beaten markers — the remains of a skeleton pointing toward a nearby tree.

"That's a strange way to mark a trail," observed Long John. "But on we go. The treasure must lie straight ahead."

"That's a strange way to mark a trail," observed Long John.

The pirates crept forward more cautiously now, torn between their greed for gold and their fear of the dead. When we were no more than 100 paces from the tree, a ghostly voice began to wail:

Fifteen bones on a dead dog's chest
Arf-arf-arf and a bottle of rum!

The cowardly scoundrels froze in their tracks, convinced that the spirit of Captain Flint was hovering nearby, but Long John simply tightened his grip on my leash, dragging me forward and urging his mates on.

"Aye, that's a familiar voice," he sniffed, "but it isn't Flint's."

And then, in a whisper that only I could hear, he added, "I smell an ill wind ahead. You and I had best look out for each other, my dear friend."

With that, we stepped into a clearing and tumbled into a large hole where a vast treasure had once been buried. Caught in a tangle of fangs and fur, Long John's crew was outraged by this discovery and directed their anger at the wily old pirate captain.

"You promised us tons of gold," one snarled, aiming a pistol at us. "But now all we have is you and a hole and that blasted pup . . ."

Their threat was interrupted — and our lives were spared — by several musket shots and the maniacal laugh of old Ben Gunn.

"I've spent three long years digging up this treasure, Mr. Silver," cried the mad hermit as he emerged from the bushes with Squire Trelawney and Dr. Livesey. "And now these good dogs have offered me passage home."

Caught in a tangle of fangs and fur, Long John's crew was outraged.

Breaking free of Long John, I rushed to Dr. Livesey, thanking him for rescuing me and begging forgiveness at the same time.

"You've saved me, sir, although I'm not sure I deserve your efforts," I whimpered. "I've been so reckless with all our lives. That cursed map almost killed us all. And I abandoned the ship and allowed myself to be captured . . ."

But the doctor waved my confessions aside and hugged me.

"Young Hawkins, you made us rich beyond our dreams when you found that map," he proclaimed. "Why, you have saved our lives at every turn. You discovered the plot, recruited Ben Gunn to our cause, then stole the ship out from under Long John Silver's nose.

"You left home an untrained pup but will return a hero," he added.

And then, as we ambled down the hillside with our prisoners, the doctor and the squire explained how Ben Gunn had convinced them to leave the stockade for the comfort of his treasure-filled den, where they could prepare a final ambush when Long John followed the treasure map to the empty pit.

On the way back to the ship, we stopped at the den so that I could see the treasure trove. It was a cavern the size of a ship's hold, filled with gold and silver bars, jewelry, coins and trinkets.

"But it's all yours now," cackled Gunn. "In return, of course, for a berth aboard your lovely schooner."

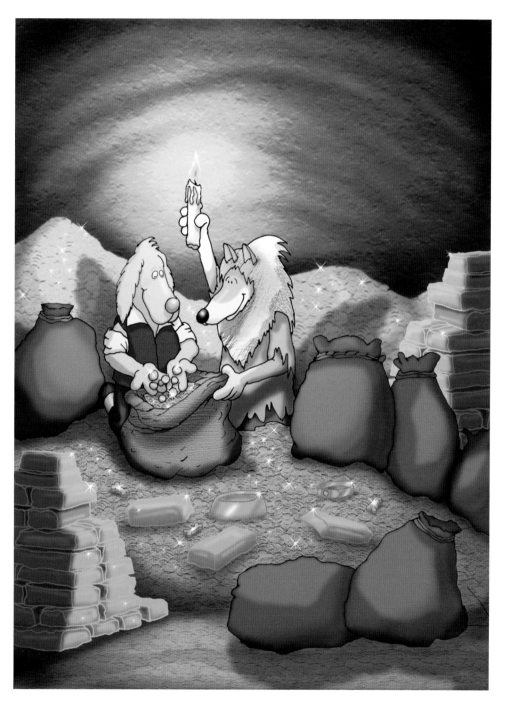

"It's all yours now," cackled Gunn. "In return for a berth aboard your schooner."

It took us two weeks to load the treasure aboard the *Hispaniola,* and even then, we had to leave a fortune in silver bars behind for lack of space. Few of the pirates had survived their adventure, and we marooned those who had with a bit of food — and the map they had wanted so desperately.

I persuaded my friends to bring Long John with us, for he had spared my life at the stockade, but his gratitude was short-lived. Fearing a trial back home, he slipped away late one night in a longboat with a bag of gold. I assume that he found his way to some tropical port and is still charming and deceiving every stranger he meets.

We gave Ben Gunn a generous share of gold but feared that he would not invest it wisely. I later heard that he had lived to a ripe old age but ended up a penniless guard dog at a small estate down the coast.

The rest invested our fortunes wisely enough that none of us has wanted for food or comfort. But although I have tried mightily to rid myself of the horrors of that voyage, it haunts me still. Whenever I hear wind blowing against sails or sea surf pounding the rocks, my mind recalls that band of cutthroat pirates and their dreadful, tuneless verse:

Fifteen bones on a dead dog's chest
Arf-arf-arf and a bottle of rum!